The Tainted Gift

The Tainted Gift

A Gospel Suspense Story

Steve N. Dab'ney
and Andrew "Deck" Gray

Strategic Book Publishing and Rights Co.

Strategic Book Publishing & Rights Co., LLC
USA | Singapore
www.sbpra.com

For information about special discounts for bulk purchases, please contact Strategic Book Publishing and Rights Co. Special Sales, at bookorder@sbpra.net.

ISBN: 978-1-68181-412-4

Dedication

I'd first like to dedicate this book to my father, Erwin O. Dab'ney, Sr. He was a man who taught me there are no shortcuts in life. I love you, sir.

I also dedicate it to my mothers, Beverly and Juanita Dab'ney, who taught me the order of life: God, family, and myself.

"I am the way, the truth, and the life: no man cometh unto the father, but by me."

—John 14:6, *KJV*

Preface

Sometimes in life, we find ourselves wanting something so bad that we would go to extremes to get it. No matter what the cost, we're willing to pay any price. Nothing in life is truly free. That is what a little farm boy, named Josh, found out one day. He thought that he was getting a gift that he has always wanted, but he didn't realize that the gift wasn't free because it came with a price tag that Josh was neither willing nor ready to pay. The price could cost him not only his life but also his soul. I used to wonder what the old folks meant by "Be careful of what you ask for because you just might get it!" I think Josh has truly found the meaning of this phrase. After you finish reading this book, I believe that you'll have a better understanding of what that phrase means as well.

Chapter 1

It was a cold, moist morning on a Georgia farm in 1995 as I stepped out of our farmhouse doorway. You could almost smell the land.

I'm telling you this story because all of us dream, but when you dream, be careful, because you might get what you wish for. Boy, did I get what I asked for. I used to dream every day, hoping and praying that I might just once get my heart's desire. I would hope that God would listen to my prayer. At that moment, a sweet voice came shining through like a ray of light in a world of silence. I started to head toward that heavenly voice—the voice I hear almost every morning—only to feel a deep aching emptiness. It was tormenting me. It was the feeling of never knowing or feeling true love.

As I walked up to the window, I could see a young lady singing, and the tears in her eyes showed that she wasn't just singing to pass away the time. No, this lady was feeling the song, the love, and the joy in her music. With every note, she came alive, feeling the tone as she felt the tears rolling down her face. This lady is also my oldest sister, but I have my doubts about that and more on that later.

A musically talented family, all except yours truly can sing their hearts out even to the little ones. Mama always said that God had something better in store for me. I just couldn't see how the good Lord had bestowed a world of talent in my sisters, yet couldn't spare a little for me. As I was looking at her, she looked up and noticed that I was staring at her. My eyes were glazed, as if I didn't hear anything else. My mind had wandered as the song carried me away.

"Mom, Josh is doing it again!" she yelled. "Man! I'm tired of this. That boy is acting more like a peeping tom each day."

At that time, I was trying to reach the kitchen as if I could beat my sister's voice to the kitchen. I reached the kitchen about the same time that my mom was yelling for all of us to come and eat at the kitchen table.

"It's breakfast time, you kids! I'm not calling you again, so get your little tails in here."

All the kids came running into the small kitchen, which was just enough room for only half of us to sit, but Mrs. Woods always made room for her kids. She looked up and saw me flying from the washroom.

As I passed my mother, I looked up and saw a pair of warm tender eyes looking back at me as she said, "You out there day dreaming again, honey? The only thing that it's going to do is give you a lot of grief."

"I know, Mama, but dreaming doesn't hurt anyone."

With only a smile, she responded with a hug that followed, "I know, baby. Mama just wants the best for you."

"I just want the best for you, baby," said Kachina, my older sister, mocking Mother as she walked around to her seat at the table.

Mother yelled, "Mind your business, and sit your narrow butt down!"

Kachina reached across and pulled Mother closer to her and whispered in her ear, "Mother, all this pampering you are doing to Josh is not helping anything. All you are doing . . ."

"Just shush your mouth and don't worry about what your father and I are doing. We're trying to help your brother. You see, he feels as though he has nothing and you and your sisters have everything. You could be a real big sister and a friend."

"What? Just because he can't sing and we can, Mom, that's not right. You treat him like he's your favorite. I don't know what the others might say, but I don't think it's right."

"Are you finished?"

"Yeah," she said and turned her head sharply to face the northern part of the house.

"Look, Miss, I got you everything just because you were the oldest, but that doesn't mean that you are old enough to dictate to your father and me what to do or say. I'll be damned if I'm going to let you tell me what I should say or do in my own house."

They both stared at each other. "Look, baby, you are gifted beyond your imagination. In a few months, you'll be gone to that school of arts in New York, and we all will be very proud of you. I know Josh especially will be."

"What? Josh? Yeah right!"

"Why do you think he follows you girls around this farm?"

"Because he's a pervert."

"Watch your mouth, young lady."

"Look, Mother, I don't care. I just want you to recognize me sometimes. It seems that you care more for him than for us."

Before Mother could respond to that remark, Beverly ran off into the hallway, bumping into her father as he entered the kitchen for breakfast.

"What's that all about?" he asked.

"I wish I knew sometimes. I think these kids are going to drive me to my grave."

"Well, honey, give me a few minutes to finish my plate and I'll get the car ready."

They looked at each other for a few seconds. Everything was quiet until they both broke out into laughter. Right around the corner, Beverly stayed in the hallway to listen to the laughter that was coming from the kitchen. She didn't know why she was crying, but she did know that she hated what she was feeling. She hated what she had said in front of her mother. As her brother looked at her, she couldn't help feeling that one day her brother would forgive her, she hoped.

The next morning, everything is like the day before. The adults of the house are getting dressed for work, and the girls are getting ready for school. But for me, I'm in the barn doing my chores. My chores begin in the morning before school, but my sisters' chores start when they come home from school. As I'm pulling hay down from the top part of the barn's loft so I can feed the horses, I look out to the edge of the fence and notice a stranger standing off in field. He's wearing a pair of black trousers and a red shirt. As I take my hand and wipe the beads of sweat that was rolling into my eyes, I look again and the stranger is gone. I look all around, but all I can see is the house and the barn. No one is in sight. I thought that it must have been the heat getting to me, but it couldn't have been that, because it was still too early in the morning for that. So I scratched my head and got back to work.

The day went by rather slowly, and it was finally 2:45 p.m., and in fifteen minutes, the bell would ring. This is what every kid is waiting for. Mrs. Thorton is finishing up the Civil War, when one of the kids slides his hand in between his chair and mine. He places a pin in the back of my chair and pulls me onto the pin. I shock the class with a loud, high-pitched squeal.

Mrs. Thorton turned around and walked toward my desk and asked, “Mr. Woods, what seems to be the problem?”

As I rubbed my backside, the young boy who placed the pin stated, “Maybe he is trying to sing again, like his sisters.” I was furious and so I lunged forward and grabbed the boy around the neck. Mrs. Thorton grabbed me and demanded that I report to the detention office. I spent the last few minutes of school at the detention office staring at the wall. The bell rang and I came running out of the school, headed for home. I stopped just long enough to watch my sisters heading toward the church for choir practice. I only wished that I could attend, but I was asked not to come back after the last rehearsal.

All that I could do was run into the woods and start kicking the trees and pulling the leaves off the branches. I put my head down into my lap and began to cry. As the tears were rolling down my face, I could almost hear a faint whisper, like someone was saying “Don’t worry, your time will come very soon.”

The next day, everything is just like clockwork on the farm. Everyone is up at the first light, but the only thing that’s different, is that today is Saturday and the afternoon is our own time. It’s about two o’clock and all the ladies of the Wood’s house were at church for choir rehearsal. Dad always goes to the local pool hall. I guess that was the only way he could relax. I stayed at home and went through the music sheets, trying to fool myself into thinking that I could sing. And why not? No one else could hear me but the farm animals, and I don’t think they have much to say about this. So I let loose and hoped for the best. I started to sing but then stopped to see where the strange yelling was coming from. The farm animals gave me their response in a loud weird way.

I stop and turn to them to say, “Quiet!”

I'm always praying that my wishes will be answered, but when I open my mouth, I let out what some people think is a fog horn. I knew that I had another day of wishing again. All of a sudden, I heard that strange voice again. It was the same voice that I had heard earlier yesterday in the woods.

This time the voice tells me to, "Come to the barn, Josh." Over and over I heard, "Come to the barn, Josh." Hesitating at first, I headed to the back door, looking all around me, thinking that my sisters was playing with me. So as I started walking toward the barn door. I call out all my sisters' names—*Beverly! Kachina! Jade*! But no response.

So I slowed down my walk and headed for the front door. As I approached the barn door, I grabbed the handle, and before I could open the door, I felt someone behind me, so I turned around quickly to find that a man was standing right in front of me. Wearing black trousers and a red shirt, the man looked like John Wayne.

I stepped back and asked the gentleman, "Can I help you?"

He quickly replied, "No, Josh. What you should be saying is, 'Can you help me?'"

"Help me, sir?"

"Yes, Josh, you. That's what I am here for."

"Oh yeah? I guess the next thing you'll be telling me is that you're my fairy godfather!"

"No, but if that will make you feel better about talking to me, well, so be it. I came here to make you an offer for something you've been wishing for, for a long time."

"I'm sorry, sir. I can't have anyone here while my parents aren't home. Can you come back when they are here?"

"No, it can't wait. I have to give it to you now. I have what you want."

"Sir, what I want, you can't give it to me. Oh boy! I wish you could, but only God can grant me that wish."

"Please, like he's the only one who can grant wishes."

"What are you saying?" I asked with a strange look on my face.

"I'm just saying that I'm in a position to give you what you want, and that, my friend, is what you've been screaming for. So, now let's get on with it."

"Wait, I just need time to . . ."

"To what? Come on, this is what you've been praying for all your life, boy. Your sisters and all the other kids tease you and they talk about you behind your back. They've already been given their gift, but you were left out. Look kid, I have other . . . well, what can I call them? Oh yes, clients! There are others who need my attention right away."

"I know, sir, but I still don't know who you are. I still don't know if this is the right thing to do."

After some time of silence, the gentleman said, "Okay, okay. I have to get going so if you could make up your mind, I would really appreciate it. But if you can't, then, well, I'm a fair guy. So I'll tell you what. This is what I'm going to do. I'll give you one chance and one chance only. When you decide to take me up on my offer just call out 'Sabton' and I'll, well . . . let's just say that I'll get back to you as soon as I can. Only one chance."

In the back, I could here the family returning home from choir practice. It was just enough to make me turn my head toward the house, but when I turned back around to finish talking to the strange man, he had disappeared. I stood there stunned and confused. It seemed that time had stood still. I called out to my mother as I approached the house.

I saw my sister at the doorway and, keeping in mind what just happened, I kept quiet about the whole thing. Later, an hour had passed, and my mom was in the kitchen preparing dinner for the family. I tried to explain to her and the family what had happened today, but no one wanted to listen. Dad was too busy trying to focus on the TV just as he does every Saturday. So he could watch the fight or the ball games. Mother was trying to listen until she realized that her dinner was burning. So she told me in a strict voice that I had to go somewhere else with that nonsense because she was trying to finish dinner.

As I was leaving, I could hear my sister Beverly say, "Mom and Dad should take him to a local hospital were the crazy doctor could check him out." I began arguing with her.

At that time Father jumped up and yelled, "Boy, who do you think you are talking to? You are far from being grown, and I don't remember seeing your name on the bills last time I checked. So the next time I hear that kind of talk coming from you, I'll make sure that you'll have something to shout about. Do you understand me, mister?"

"Yes, sir."

"And you girls, what did your mother and I just finish saying to you? Especially you, Beverly? We told you to stop teasing your brother."

"Well, I really don't see what the big commotion is about. Like there aren't 100 million people out there who wish they could sing."

As he sat down to watch the fight, he told them, "You kids better get your heads out of the clouds and into the books, because no one is going to give you anything. That's why I always say that the only thing you should be stealing from this world is your education. But you kids don't listen. That's why when you hit eighteen years of age your ass is out of here."

"Oh damn you, Dan! You're always trying to scare the children and run them away from home. I don't know what you been smoking old man but no one is going to run my children out of my house."

"Your house?"

"Yes, that's right. My house, and if anyone has to go, it will be you."

"Look, you crazy lady, I will pack everything you and those kids have in a trash bag and put you out."

He then walked away, talking to himself. Then everything got quiet, and no one said anything for the rest of the night.

Chapter 2

The scene changes as we turn to a young doctor who is working at a desk in his home, and by the looks of his house, you might say that he's kind of wealthy. We see him working at the desk, moving papers around.

After a second, you could almost see the shadow of a black figure just stepping out of the darkest corner of the dimly lit room, and the first thing the gentleman hears is, "You miss me, doctor?"

With a jolt, the gentleman jumps up, tripping over the furniture, and spins around, seeing the gentleman standing right in front of him. The gentleman knew the figure's name. It's kind of funny because the strange man dressed in a red shirt and black pants never gave it to anyone, especially him. He wished to God that he didn't know the figure's name, and he wished that he had never met this man or made that stupid, outrageous wish.

But he tells himself that he has been waiting for this day for as long as he could remember, and that he is prepared. His only worry is that he hoped that his plan would work.

"I've been waiting for you."

"Oh. You have?" replied the man in the red shirt.

"Yes, I have. By the way, what is your name?"

"That is not important right now."

"Oh, I beg to differ. You see a name tells you a lot about a person. Who they are and where they come from. Don't you think so, Satan, or do you want me to call you Lu . . ."

"What? You think that I . . . that I'm . . . Yeah, yeah, whatever, but the fact is that time is up and that your dues are due."

"Well, I've been ready for this." The doctor looked smug as he walked around the desk and confronted the man in the red shirt.

"Oh, you have? Well, that's a first. Usually, they're running and screaming."

"Well, I have a surprise for you. This is a special occasion."

"Oh, I can't wait to see this. I'm scared." The man with the red shirt did a funny tremble and shake while laughing.

The scared doctor picked up the phone and asked, "Would you please come in?"

"What is that, some kind of code?"

They looked at each other. The man with red shirt smiled as he turned toward the door. The room filled with an awkward chill that no heat could warm. "What's the matter?" replied the stranger. "You seem cold and scared."

"No, it's just that I've got a few things on my mind."

"Okay, okay. I've played along long enough. I've always wanted to see from time to time if any one can best me. So let's see if you have what it takes."

"Oh, I think you will be very surprised."

"Oh, really? I love surprises."

At that time, three gentlemen walk in. "So, what's this? You all are going to try to kill me?" the man in the red shirt said.

"No," replied the young doctor. "I know that is stupid and that's not how I pictured myself resolving this unique situation."

"Yes," replied the man in the red shirt. "But unique for you not for me. Isn't that right? So what's this special plan you have that's going to get you out of this deal?"

"Look closer and you will see what I'm talking about," replied the young doctor.

The man took a closer look and realized what he was seeing was very strange. "I don't believe this, but this is a first."

What he was seeing was clones—identical copies of the young doctor. Usually they ask to live forever or beg for more time. But never this.

"Well, what are we going to do now? I know what I'm going to do and that is retire for the evening with a glass of my best wine and a nice juicy steak, because if you can't take the right person you can't take anyone. So good evening, my not-so-bright friend. Go scare someone else with theatrical drama."

"Wait," responded the man in the red shirt, "you're partly right. But I know something that you don't know. He started to prance around with a joyful step in his walk.

"Oh yeah?" The doctor's face went pale and the tone of his voice drop. "What's that?"

"That, my dear sir is that, at the time of the original deal you were one person and that means no matter how many times you slice and dice yourself, the deal still goes and now that I have four all together, and that makes me so, so happy."

"What do you mean?"

"Oh boy, let me explain this to you in a different way that you kids can understand."

The stranger reached around his back and pulled out a large bowl of white milk. "Let's say that there is a bowl of milk and you contaminate it with blood." A cut appeared on his hand and blood dripped into the bowl. "But you decided to separate it into three bowls. You see, there are three bowls floating in mid air with contaminated blood in them, but the milk is still contaminated with the blood no matter how many times you split the bowl. Well, you see, when you contaminated yourself with our deal you tried to deceive me by cloning yourself, thinking that if I can't decide who made the original deal, then I would be forced to release you from our deal. Not! All you did was contaminate the rest of your new brothers and sweeten the pot for me."

The clones turned and look at one another. The first one turned to the doctor who started this and replied, "You condemned us all, you son of a bitch!"

"What? You thought that we didn't know about what you were doing? What is it with you so-called people? You want to play with fire, but you don't want to get burnt."

All of a sudden, the man's eyes started to glow and his skin started to change color. "You all wanted to make a deal with us, but when it's time to pay us our dues, you cheat and scheme against us so you don't have to pay the piper. Then they say that we are evil."

Suddenly, the room goes dim. The clones all run toward the door. When they get to the front door, a dark creature comes out of the shadows. They turn around and the creature's tentacles grab them. Once the figure touches them, they also turn into dark slim figures.

You could hear the screams of torment from all of the victims that came before, as its gates opened up, and just as quickly as it started, it ends.

"Now, doctor, it's your turn. What? No screaming? I thought by now that you'd be begging and kicking, and there would be a little bit of screaming."

The doctor quickly picks up a cross and thrusts it in front of the man.

"Oh no, wrong story, asshole. Shit! We gave you brains, and this is what you came up with? I need to talk to someone about this cross stuff. Now back to business. Where were we? Oh yeah, you owe me and now I've come to collect."

As he raised his hand, the room glowed with a strange red radiance as the darkness came and consumed the doctor.

He made one statement as he was disappearing: "You can't win forever and one day . . ." The doctor's voice fades as he enters the void, and just as quickly as it started, it was over.

The room was bright, and the door is now opening up again.

As the man turns to head out the door, he whispers, "He put a cross in my face. Ha-ha, a cross! Boy, what's next? Garlic? I can see it now. 'Stop or I'll destroy you with this garlic!' What they need to do is shove it up their ass. Ha-ha." He laughed as he ventured on.

Chapter 3

The scene changes to a bar. There's a nervous woman sitting at the bar. Her hands are shaking as she takes another puff from her cigarette. She's watching her watch as well as the door. She noticed a strange man about six-foot and two inches tall with black hair and wearing a grey two-piece suit. She turned to the door and then back to the man in the suit, who is still looking at her. This time he gives her a wink from his left eye. She tried not to pay attention, but when he walked over and offered to pay for her drinks, sitting down next to her, she found herself in a position that was very uncomfortable and hard to get out of, so he politely introduced himself as Sam and she replied as Melissa.

As time went by, they both found themselves still holding a warm conversation that went on till closing. He also noticed that she has relaxed and opened up, so he offered to walk her home. At first she refused, but he was determined to hear her say yes. He stated that it was late and a lady like her should be escorted home. She looked at him with a little bit of hesitation, but she finally agreed. As they walked down the Rue of New Orleans, the two acted as though they were no longer strangers. As the night went on, so did the conversation that sparked a relationship with these two lonely hearts.

"So, Sam, tell me, who were you waiting for, or what?"

"I believe it was you."

"Ha-ha. Nice reply."

"Well, the truth is, it was a blind date, but she never showed. You know how those blind dates can be. Besides, I'm not a person who enjoys surprises. Do you?" As they walked through the streets of the French Quarters, the young lady looked up and noticed that she was back at her hotel. She turned to him as she put on a warm smile.

She opened the front door of the hotel and said, "I would invite you in, but . . ."

"No, no. I understand."

"Please, I just have a few things on my mind right now and being with someone new for a one-nighter is not what I need right now."

"I understand." He leaned over to kiss her, and she responded as if she'd been waiting for this all night. She handed Sam a piece of paper. He took it and put it in his pocket without looking at it. She thought to herself, *I wonder if he's going to call. If not, it wouldn't be the first.*

As he stepped down from the platform, he gave her another kiss in hopes that it'll keep her until she sees him again. As they said their goodbyes, she waited out on the step until she couldn't see Sam any longer. With a smile, she couldn't believe that at a time like this and in such a short time, she would've started to feel something for someone, hoping that it one day could be something more.

The next morning, the phone rang and Melissa reached up from under the covers to grab the phone. She glanced at the clock by her bed. It was 8:45 a.m.

She said, "This better be good."

"I hope so," replied the person on the other end. "I was wondering if we could get together and have lunch, maybe a picnic, or if it's too early, maybe dinner later."

"No, no, a picnic is fine."

"Okay, I'll pick you up in front of your door in about an hour."

"How about two hours? You know us women."

"Yeah, I do."

"Okay, in two hours I'll be ready."

"Okay, bye."

"Bye." She jumped up as if she had a fire lit under her. Not slowing down to take her clothes off as she made her way into the shower, she slammed the shower door still half-dressed with her nightgown on. It was going to be a busy day. She had so much to do and not enough time in one day to do it all.

While the day progressed, she couldn't help thinking about Sam. Then she realized that in about forty-five minutes he would be at her doorstep. She quickly started searching her purse for the crumpled piece of paper that had Sam's number. She called him to see if it could be changed to dinner around 7:30 p.m. Much to her surprise, Sam was very understanding and agreed.

***

Melissa was waiting outside. She looked with an urgent face for Sam. A black Porsche pulled up. She looked at it with approval. She was excited, and she felt as though she was so lucky that this guy walked into her life. She tried not to show her excitement as Sam got out of the vehicle to open the car door for her. She made her way into the car not knowing what the night would bring. Melissa and her mystery man, Sam, were seen as a couple at one of the elegant restaurants in the New Orleans downtown area. His plans were working out just right. He noticed the look on her face as he was trying to make a good impression with her.

It was well after the dinner hour by now, and most of the customers are gone. The only people who were still there were

Melissa and Sam. As they talked over a glass of white Chablis and a piece of cheesecake, the bill arrived.

When they finally got into the car, she leaned over and asked, "What's next?"

"Well, I would love to take you for a beautiful carriage ride thought the French Quarters."

As she got positioned in her seat, she looked at him with a warm soft glance, and said, "Well, we could go back to your place and finish this perfect evening."

He just smiled and turned to start the car. As he drove off, you could see and hear the car burning rubber as he left the parking area. She gave a wild look and started to laugh.

The couple went to his place, finishing the piece of cheesecake that they brought with them. He opened another bottle of wine.

She said, "This would be a lot more fun if we had this in the bedroom."

As they kissed, she started to pull off her clothes. Sam replied by doing the same. While they lay there on the bed, he hesitated at first as he looked into her eyes.

She asked, "What's the matter?"

"Nothing," replied Sam. He began to touch and kiss her breasts. At the same time, she slowly started to touch him, letting her hand wander and move slowly down his stomach. She gently kissed him on his chest. The room was dimly lit with the light of a candle flickering in the background, showing a shadow figure on the wall. You could see Sam moving closer and closer as he started to kiss Melissa down her legs. As she moaned, he anxiously ripped off her panties. She wiggled as though she was trying to get from underneath him, but then she finally stopped and gave in to him. He kissed her on the lips, as if he was waiting for her to do something that would let him know if he was on the right track.

She began to kiss him down on his stomach and thighs and finally she saw his face as she reached a spot that would only get the response that she was looking for. As he tried not to make a sound, he couldn't help it. He screamed out in a high-pitched sound. She looked at him eye-to-eye and she giggled.

Then she grabbed his head and jammed his face into her breasts, saying, "No, baby, you're not finished yet." He sucked on her breasts until his jaw was tired, and he just couldn't suck anymore.

Then Melissa went on top. She was riding back and forth—just like riding a horse. She grasped harder to his arms, and then she pulled at the hair on his chest. At the moment of climax, she dug her nails into his arms, and a black fluid came out. The gentleman noticed this, but when he looked at her, her eyes were closed. So he rubbed his arm, wiping the fluid away.

An hour later, as she was resting in his arms, she turned to him and said, "It's been a long time since anyone made me feel this way. I do mean a long time."

"Well, we have to change that," Sam replied as he leaned over to kiss her, seemingly trying to start the heated moment all over again.

But she stopped him, saying, "As fun as this has been, I must get down to business. But since you made me feel so good, I'll try not to let you suffer. Her voice was getting deeper as if she was possessed. Sam looked up as he opened his eyes wider with confusion and fear. He moved backward toward one end of the bed thinking it was no use to run. He felt some kind of force pulling and stretching him across the bed, spreading his arms and legs, as she stood at the foot of the bed. A large black hole appeared, and in this, you could see something was stirring.

While this was going on, she slowly started to morph back into a man. "Oh yes, I'm a man. Surprise!"

After the transformation, Sam screamed as the tentacles from the black hole were getting closer. As they latched onto the man's body, he yelled out, "It's not my time, you son of bitch! I still have a little more time left."

"No, you don't. If you had read your contract, in fine print at the bottom of the last page on the back, it has the due date, and you are way past the due date. You were trying to stay under our radar. I have you good. For the defense, I have a nice snapshot collection of the deed being done."

As the stranger talked, you could see the blood being drained right from his body. You could still see somewhat of a skeleton talking.

"You lying son of a bitch."

"Oh, why did you have to spoil this special moment between us now? I guess you won't be calling . . . ha-ha. All bets are off!"

At that moment you could see the skeleton of a man. His eyes went wide as two eye sockets drained and pulled into the skull, and then small creatures came out of the black hole and started to eat the guy as he screamed and yelled in torment.

"What?" replied the stranger in the red shirt and black pants. "You didn't mind it when you were eating me earlier. Boy, you guys are never satisfied." He laughed. As the room faded out, so did everything else along with it.

The next morning, the housekeeper arrived as she always did every morning to clean up the mess that occurred the night before. As she stepped into the bedroom, she stopped and looked. The housekeeper looked as one would look at a jar with a dead animal inside, while trying to analyze what the hell it was. She tried to scream. She took a deep breath, and at the instant she screamed, she also ran. She was yelling in Spanish and ran right past a police officer, who was passing in front of the room, eating his hot dog.

One hour later, the apartment where the dark, bloody incident occurred was filled with the city's police officers, detectives, and medical examiner.

A police officer turned to one of the detectives and asked, "What do you think happened here, Sir?"

"I don't know, and I have a strange feeling that I don't want to know."

They turned their attention to the front door where a police officer was trying to get the housekeeper to come back into the apartment to get her statement and identification of some of the stranger's belongings, but all the housekeeper was doing was kicking and biting the police officer on the arm.

"Sir, she just won't come back into this apartment," replied the police officer. "I could mace her and drag her through the door if you would like for me to."

The detective gave the police officer a strange look and said, "Do you want me to mace you and drag you back to your ex-wife?"

The detective turned and said in a low voice, "Asshole." He turned to the patrol officer next to him and said, "Take her down to the station for questioning and have the crime scene boys come and take pictures as soon as possible. Get them to me fast as you can. I mean like yesterday."

"Yes, Sir."

Before the picture faded, you could see what was left of his body—all black, burnt and charred.

Chapter 4

Back on the farm, Josh came running out of the house as he heard a loud commotion coming from within. You could hear Josh's mother and father screaming as Josh sat next to his younger sister, Kachina.

She put her arm on her brother and said, "Don't worry, I believe in you." With teary eyes, they held each other and watched the stars.

Josh pulled back and said to his little sister Kachina, "I'm going to do it."

"What? Do what?"

He stood up, and then said, "I'm going to do it."

"Oh yeah. Do what?" cried his sister.

"I'm going to get my wish."

Josh ran into the fields that were directly behind the house. He ran hard and fast, until he figured that he was in the middle of the fields. Out of breath, he kneeled down on the ground trying to catch his breath. When he was finally rested, he looked straight up and asked if this was what he really wanted. He started to cry, asking for advice but there wasn't any.

So he yelled, "Don't you leave me, too! Okay, I'll just do what I have to do. I'm ready. You hear me? Sabton! I said that I'm ready! Now!"

Time passed by and Josh sat on a crate in the cold night. As you could see the light go out at the house, Josh got up with a limp from sitting too long. He headed back home, walking slowly with his head hanging low like he had nothing left inside.

***

The next morning, Josh was in the barn doing his chores and cleaning the stalls out. As he threw another fork full of straws in the corner of the stall, he heard a small whistling noise. As he kept going with his work, he saw that the horses were uncomfortable and moving around. The whistling was getting louder and louder. When finally, he turned toward the door thinking that someone was coming into the barn door, he felt a cold touch on his right shoulder.

"Hi, Josh, I'm back like I said I would. But you called me sooner than I guessed."

While Josh was stunned, he looked at the stranger's face. He said, "I thought you had forgotten about me."

"No Josh, I just had to take care of some unfinished business, but I told you that I'll be back and here I am, like I said I would. Ta-da."

He froze, waiting for Josh to say something. "So where were we? Oh yeah, I could help make your dreams come true, Josh, for the right price. My dad always said that everyone wants something for something, and I know that you're not here from the Salvation Army. Oh you little, little con artist. Look Josh, if you want me to go I'll just leave, but before I go, let's say I'll give it to you on a trial basis."

"What do you have in mind?" asked Josh.

"Well, let's just say that it's a temporary gift."

"What do you mean a temporary gift?" Josh cried out.

"Just like I said, it's a gift."

"How does this gift work?" You could see Josh's eyes getting wide as all resistance was fading away.

"Well, when I give it to you I'm going to leave for a while, and when I return, I will give you the opportunity to keep the gift. Or I'll let you perform one task, and if you don't complete this task to the best of your ability, you must keep the gift."

"It's a trick of some kind. I know it is!" yelled Josh.

"No, no. It's something that you could do now."

"Oh yeah! What is it?"

"Ahh . . . no, no. Not yet. You'll know soon enough."

"What is this is all about?"

"Let's shake on it."

Josh pulled his hand up and reached for the stranger's hand.

As soon as his index finger touched the stranger's hand, he felt a shock that made him pull away quickly.

"Oh, it must be this dry heat," smiled the man in the red shirt.

"Not like any dry heat that I've seen before," Josh replied.

"Oh, shut up and shake my hand, damn it."

This time when Josh grabbed his hand with hesitation, there was a strong light—a weird kind of light—cold and dark, and when he opened his eyes, the stranger was gone. Josh looked around and yelled out, but the stranger was nowhere to be found. Josh didn't know what to do. He sat there wondering how, when, and what to do. He was more scared and confused than curious. He closed his eyes and grasped his hands. He felt a cold chill come over him.

He opened his mouth, and the voice that came out wasn't his. Or was it? He paused. As tears rolled down his face, he never knew that it would feel this good coming out. He hit every high note with a greatest of ease. He opened his eyes as he kept singing. As he spun around, he saw his mother standing in the doorway. He stopped and looked back at his mother as she dropped her basket of eggs, collapsed to her knees, and passed out on the barn floor.

All that Josh could do was just stare at his mother for a few seconds, and then he said, "Hey Mom, I can sing! Mom! Mom! Oh, Mom! Oh, Mom! Oh boy!"

When Josh's mother came to, she went to the kitchen to sip on a glass of cold water.

Beverly was helping her mother as she said, "Take it slow, Mom."Their mom took one taste of the water and tossed it aside. She reach behind the counter and she pulled out a small bottle of gin, as the father tried to get past his children to his wife.

"What happened, honey?" he asked.

With her eyes as big as goose eggs, and at the same time still trying to drink all the gin as fast as she could, she tried to tell her family what she saw in the barn. She pointed to Josh and tried to say his name. The family looked over to the doorway where Josh was standing, looking at his family.

"What in the hell did you do now, boy? I am sick and tired of you moping around here thinking that you can play on our emotions. Well, boy, I'm about to show you a whole lot of emotions."

Their father pulled out his belt, but Mother reached up to grab her husband. She missed his shirtsleeve though. All the children egged the father on to give Josh the whipping that they thought he deserved, but their mother quieted her family down and stopped her husband at the same time. She knew that no one was listening to her. Thinking that she was still in shock, she looked at Josh, trying to tell him to sing. But the noise level was still too high. The children were still pushing and nudging their father to whip their brother.

Finally, the mother yelled for Josh to sing, and suddenly, the whole room was quiet, and all you could hear were the sweet notes as Josh enlightened every melody. You could see everyone was amazed. The father snatched the bottle of gin and a second bottle of Jack Daniels. He tried to sit in the chair that his wife was just in, but he just slid to the floor. Soon, as Josh was finished singing, his little sisters all ran to him and started rubbing his neck as if they could find the reason why Josh was able to sing so beautifully. As Josh gave a big smile, he noticed all but one of his sister's was basking in the joy of his great gift. Beverly couldn't find the pride or the emotion that could make her run to her brother's side and take part in his enjoyment. As he stared at her, she also stared back. Neither one said a word.

Next, the father said, "Oh boy. He's going to make us rich. I can see it now."

"Wait a minute!" cried out their mother to her outrageous husband. "This is not ours to give, or to keep. This is all Josh's decision."

Once again the room got quiet, and everyone waited to hear what Josh had to say. He looked at the eyes of his siblings with pride and smugness.

He said, "I have a gift that I should be giving and sharing with the world."

His father jumped up and down, saying, "Yes! Oh yessss!"

Mother only replied, "I hope we're doing the right thing, and by the way, how did all of this happen anyway?"

"Oh, woman, it's his change. You know, becoming a man and all."

"I don't know, honey. I have a strange feeling about this."

The picture faded and you could see Josh and his sister lock eyes once again. Beverly turned away. Josh wasn't sure, but he believed that he saw his sister cry for the first time.

***

The next day was Sunday morning, and everyone was at church. The pastor was just finishing up the sermon. He asked the church choir to come forth and end the service with a song. The organ played, and the music filled the air. Once the choir started to sing, you could see Josh stirring in his chair, like a balloon about to pop.

Anxious, his mother looked over and leaned toward Josh and said, "Easy, Son, there's a time and place. This not the place." It was as if he was waiting for the right moment.

The choir was singing "That's When He Blessed Me." It was the moment that Josh had been waiting for. He got up from the back aisle where he was sitting. His mother signaled for him to sit down, but this was what he had been waiting for all of his life, and he hoped that his parents would understand that he had to do this. Looking over at his mother, he could see her gesturing a signal for him to sit down, but he was more confused to see his father thrusting his hand upward, gesturing him to stand and sing. His mother noticed it and grabbed her husband's hand to stop him. On the last stanza, Josh stepped in and took over the lead singer's position. His voice hit all the high notes. Even a few that nobody ever hit before. The church was so amazed, and half the congregation didn't know whether to ask the boy to sit down or keep singing. When they saw that a few people were standing, his mother included, and clapping him on, the rest of the congregation joined in. The song ended and everyone clapped and cheered for Josh.

The church service was over; the pastor was greeting the visitors at the entrance of the church, as they departed for the day. As the congregation was leaving, he stopped Josh and his parents saying, "Well, Son, that performance was breathtaking. Just next time, let the music director know in advance. I think Sister Trenice was very upset about what you did."

"I know, sir, but I felt I had to just come out, and once my spirit heard the gospel, I just couldn't help myself."

The pastor and the group stopped just enough to see Sister Trenice pass them and hear her upset reply of "Hummm."

Josh's father said, "Well, if you could sing, then my son wouldn't have to do your job."

Mother kept trying to stop her husband. "Please, stop it. Leave that woman alone." They all looked at Sister Trenice.

While she looked back, she said, "Well I never . . ."

"Well, that's why you can't sing!" Josh's father cried out.

Josh's mother yelled to her husband, "Stop it! You're embarrassing all of us here and in the church, and not only that, but you are disrespecting the church and Pastor Erwin."

"No, that's all right. I really want to talk to you about Josh singing in our church choir."

"Well, I don't know if that will be a good idea. See, sir, what I'm saying is that I'm on bad terms with a few of the choir members, and think that I should just leave all the singing to Sister Trenice and the music director."

"Well, if you change your mind about this, let me know, Son. I would love to hear your voice coming from the choir stand."

As Mother walked closer to her son, she asked, "Are you sure that this is what you want to do?"

"Well, I'm not really sure, but I'll know if I walked back in the church for rehearsal. I have a funny feeling that I'll be where I belong."

"I know what you mean."

"You do?"

"Yeah! What? Just because I had all of you that don't mean that I can't keep an eye on you from time to time."

"I know, Mother."

"I want to tell you that I will always love you and . . ."

"I know that, Mom. I know that."

As the family gathered at the car, Josh looked at his oldest sister with a relentless face and asked, "What's your problem?"

She just looked and got into the old beat-up pick-up truck, saying, "Show off."

As the family got into the truck, their dad pulled Josh closer to him as to hug him.

***

Early Tuesday morning, Josh is practicing on different songs to see if he had a limit of a certain range of key notes, but he didn't. He could sing any song on any key at different levels. The barn door swung opened and Josh looked up only to see his oldest sister, Beverly, walking toward him at a fast pace.

"What's your problem?"

"Snap, Josh, Dad will be home in an hour and you still haven't got your work done."

"I will. I just needed to practice a little."

"Practice? That's all you do now is practice. You know I'm tired of all the crap that you have everyone believing in. Well, I'm not going to be fooled."

"What's wrong, big sister? You can't take the competition? Ohhhh, I see, you want to be the only one with the fame and glory. Well, is big sister so afraid that I'm going to take her thunder and fame away, or her scholarship from the school of performance arts? Is that it? Are you afraid that I'm going to take mother's love away from you? Yes, that's it. Isn't it? Tell me."

"Hell no!"

"Yes, it is. Admit it. Why does it bother you so much anyway, big sister? When I was in grief with my problems and you were basking in the glow of your great, bright fortune did I say anything? No, although you wanted the glory and the fame all for yourself. Why can't we ever share everything? I mean like Mom's love."

"It's only because you want everything, Josh—Mom's love and the glory of your new gift. Where the hell did you get it anyway? That's still a mystery, but that's between you and God. You are a spoiled brat who wants Mom and Dad to always cry over you! Or you do want to be in the spotlight? Either way, you are going to get your way."

"Well, we all can't be stuck-up selfish little bitches like you, Sis."

Beverly turned to her brother and slapped him in the face. He fell back against the wall. After rubbing his face for a second, he pulled himself up, charged at his sister, and punched her in the head. The fight progressed further, and then there came a knock on the front door of the house. Their younger sister, Jade opened the door. She looked at the stranger at the door as he looked back at her.

"Well, little one, are your parents home?" he asked as a loud noise of breaking glass was heard all the way from the back of the house. The gentleman tried to see past the crack of the door to find out where the noise originated from; it seemed that his only problem was dealing with the child that blocked him.

"Well, can you tell your mother or father that Mr. Gray from Star Entertainment is here to see them about an important matter, your brother?" The young girl stopped staring long enough to yell out her brother's name.

"Josh, it's for you!" The two siblings stopped fighting in a mid punch and stared at each other. Both of their faces were covered with bruises and a little bit of blood. His sister repeated that the gentleman was there to see him. Josh ran out to the porch with torn clothes and looked at the nicely dressed gentleman.

He approached the gentleman and asked, "Are you here to see me, Sir?"

"Well, yes, but I need to talk to your parents first. Are they home?"

"Oh yeah. Wait here."

Josh ran out the back door and into the fields that were located right behind the house. He first ran up to his father, who was working the land. Josh was trying to catch his breath.

"Da . . . Da . . . d . . . there's a . . . man . . . Wan . . . to . . . see . . . you."

"Boy, what in the cow crap are you saying?"

"Honey, give the boy time to catch his air."

Once Josh caught his breath, he told his parents about the strange man that wanted to see them as they walked back to the house. The family was in the house sitting down. Mother and Father were in the front room talking to the man who was still a mystery to them all.

"Boy, what did you do now?"

His oldest sister looked on as she made a face of disapproval, thinking that she knew what was going on and that she didn't like it. Josh looked over at his big sister, and then he stopped to give her a warm smile to let her know that he had no hard feelings about what happened earlier today.

He noticed that she refused to give any type of emotions. Instead, she frowned at him and said, "Jerk."

Josh replied, "Since you feel that way, don't forget that I still need to finish that butt-whooping you got coming." His oldest sister turned around to comment on her brother's remark, but their father came into the room.

He said, "Josh we need to see you in the front room now."

When Josh passed his sister, he gave her a look that made his father push him into the room, which caused him to stumble across the floor. He caught himself before tumbling to the floor. His mother told to him to have a seat.

"This is Mr. Gray from the entertainment business, and he wants you to sign a contract with him to sing professionally."

"Wait a minute. I said that I wanted to hear him sing first, before I put any money or time in this. No one just walks off the street and . . ."

"Wait now one minute, Mr. Gray. My boy can sang, and we don't need no city tightass, dark-suit-wearing mother . . ."

"Honey!" yelled Josh's mother. "I'm sorry that my husband is such an idiot. Please tell me how you heard about our son Josh's newfound ability."

"Deacon Kelly is my oldest son. He gave me a call yesterday about this newfound voice he heard at church."

"Yes, we know Deacon Kelly. He a good man, but sir, still, our first concern is to our son, and I hope you can understand why my husband feels the way that he does."

"I do understand. I have children of my own, and once in a while I become over-protective about them, too. All I want is to see for myself whether I can give Josh the full support that he needs on this. Now, sir, if this was your job, you would do the same thing."

"Yeah, I guess."

"So, Josh, how do you feel about singing for me and your parents?"

"Okay, I guess, Sir."

"Well, let's hear you, Son."

Josh tilted his head up toward the ceiling as if he was trying to gather all of his feelings in one big burst. Once the first note broke the silence, Mr. Gray leaned forward, staring at Josh.

When the concert was over, Mr. Gray jumped to his feet, signaling his hands toward Josh, saying, "More! I want to hear more, please."

Mr. Gray rushed to pull his briefcase open and began to go through his paperwork. Finally he pulled out a small stack of papers and turned them toward Josh's father and mother.

"This a contract, and I would like for my company to represent Josh."

"I don't know. This sure is a lot of reading to do before we sign anything."

"Okay, okay. I'll give you some time, but please give my company a chance before you look anywhere else, okay?"

Josh's mother looked at her husband and nodded. "We need to talk this over and find out what is best for Josh . . ."

"And the family!" yelled the father.

"Okay, I truly understand. I will be in touch, and please, give us a try. Thank you."

The gentleman left and the attention turned back to the family as they discussed what the next steps for Josh would be.

***

The next day Josh was out back behind the barn practicing a couple of songs. Before, he could never finish a song because he felt that there was no reason since his voice sounded the way it did. Now he was cramming in years of music in one afternoon. Although he knew that it was impossible, he still had to try. The barn door swung opened, and Josh looked through the crack of the barn wall to see what the commotion was all about. His youngest sister and his mother were calling for him. Josh got up and ran toward the barn door to see what all the yelling was about.

"Your father and I have decided to let you sign with Mr. Gray, but only if that's what you want. So it's all up to you."

"Well, Mom, this has been my dream for as long as I can remember, so I guess so."

"Well, that solves that problem. We are going to call Mr. Gray and tell him the good news."

His mother walked back into the house. Josh just stood there wondering if he had made the right choice, and when all of this would end or if it even would. He thought of the strange man in the red shirt and black trousers.

***

The next day, Mr. Gray showed up and laid out a series of papers.

"Well, I don't know about this, and I do believe that we need a lawyer to decipher all this legal jargon."

"Well," Mr. Gray said, "I'm not going to cheat you or Josh. To show that I'm on the same level, I'll tell you what I'm going to do. The first five shows are on me. What I'm saying is that I will foot the whole bill for the arrangement of the concert hall and everything else. You don't have to pay for anything, and you aren't committed to anything. There isn't a bidding contract, and I'm going to give you half of what we take in. Is that a deal or what?"

"Well, I guess that's fair. What you think, honey?"

"Whatever Josh wants is okay with me."

They turned to Josh to see him standing there with a big smile on his face, and that was all his mother and father needed. The next week, Josh was backstage preparing for his first live performance in a nearby town. You could see that his mother was watching him closely. When the time was near, she stepped up to him from behind.

She whispered to him, "You know you can go home if you want to. No one can make you go through with this except for you."

Josh turned to his mother with tears in his eyes. He gave her a kiss and whispered, "I know."

Then he stepped out on stage. The audience got quiet. Josh walked up to the microphone and look out into the audience. He thought that he saw the man in the red shirt, but when he looked again, he thought to himself that he was seeing things. He closed his eyes for a moment, and then he opened his mouth. The next thing that you heard were the sweetest sounds to ever come from someone's voice. The crowd watched in amazement.

Josh opened his eyes as the notes shouted emotional feelings loudly. He looked at the audience and felt a strong, warm rush of emotions flowing out of him. The crowd jumped to their feet, and with loud claps, gave their approval. Josh gave a strong, sweet smile to the crowd as a tear rolled down his face. From out the corner of his eye, he could see that his mother was in the shadows holding tight to her husband. While they listened, tears rolled down her face. The song ended, and the crowd cheered for more and screamed for Josh to continue on. But Josh was so overwhelmed with the response that he had received, he completely froze up on the stage not knowing what to do. Snapping out of it, he walked off the stage. He looked over his shoulder, and still wondered how long would all of this would last. He exited the stage and fell into the arms of his awaiting mother, who was waiting offstage in the shadows of the background.

As Josh looked up into his mother's eyes, he felt drained and weak. He felt that he was losing himself. He told her that he was so scared.

"I know, baby. I felt the same way when I saw you up there singing your heart out."

Before anyone knew it, a large crowd had surrounded Josh as he tried to hang on to his mother.

Mr. Gray rushed to Josh saying, "What's wrong with you? Get back out there."

"Mr. Gray, how could you be so cold? Don't you see that the boy needs a few minutes to pull himself together?"

"Okay, okay, I'm sorry. Listen, Josh, take your time, and when you are ready, well, you let us know." Josh wasn't ready for all of this and seeing people arguing over him wasn't how he figured that it would be. All he wanted was to go home.

"Mom, I want to leave." The people refused to listen to anyone else except for the elegant sounds that came from the little boy on the stage. Josh decided to sing part of another song, and then he stopped to look around. He hesitated and looked out at the crowd. He dropped the microphone and ran off stage. Suddenly, he was gone. While the music was playing, he started to look around for an easy way out. Once the opportunity arose, he ran out to the truck's tailgate. Taking a deep breath, he leaned against the tail-end and began to try to collect his thoughts.

As soon as he thought he was ready to maybe go back inside, he heard someone say, "Well, looks like you bit off more than you can chew, or should I say sing? Whatever it is, it seems to me that you are in a bind."

Josh looked at the stranger in the red shirt. He yelled out, "What do you want from me?"

"Come on now, Son. You know what I want, and it's not from you any longer. I think it's time to pay the piper." Josh looked toward the ground as he tried to solve a puzzle.

He whispered to himself, "Wait a minute, I know who you are. I remember now."

The stranger in the red shirt looked at Josh. "What's the matter? You're mad because you have to give the devil his dues?"

Josh's eyes went wide, as if he had seen the walking dead appear right in front of him.

The stranger looked at Josh and said, "I'm going to give you a freebie. I'll give you a little more time to either enjoy my thoughtful gift or prepare yourself for my return. Either way I will be back. See, I still have some unfinished business to take care of. I thought that I would just drop in to see how my investment was coming along. So until then, I will be watching you, Josh." Then the stranger faded into the dark shadows just as quickly as he had appeared.

In the middle of all the commotion, no one ever noticed that Josh had left, until his mother started looking for him. Everyone began to fan out to find him. Getting her thoughts together, Josh's' mom went right to the spot where she knew her little boy would be.

"Well, I figured that you might be here, and then I thought that we could get out of here. Just as soon as your father gets out here."

"Mom?"

"Yes, honey?"

"I'm afraid, and I want to tell you something that happened some months ago."

"Well, honey, what is it? You can tell me."

Josh tried to form his mouth to pronounce the words, but as soon he found the courage to tell her, there was a voice yelling, "What in the name of the stars are you two doing out here when everyone's looking for you both?"

"Well, honey, we'll talk again soon."

***

The next day started as quickly as the night ended. Josh's sister passed by his room to see him sitting, facing the wall.

"What's wrong?" Silence hit the wall and bounced back again. "What's wrong?"

"Look, I'm sorry that I . . . I . . .well, you know about the way that I blew up at you the other day . . . I guess that I was . . . you know, jealous of you and everything."

"I wasn't trying to take your pie. All I wanted was a piece for me."

"I know, but I've been in the spotlight for so long, and I guess I'm not ready to give it up yet. But I've learned one thing, and that is I will always have a career. But I only have one brother."

She smiled as she looked at her brother. She hoped that things could be different with them. He looked at his sister and a smile formed across his face. She reached out for her brother as he ran into her open arms. The moment passed, and he looked down at the floor. He was still in his sister's arms.

He said, "Well, I won't be bothering you much longer anyway."

"What do you mean by much longer? Mr. Gray hasn't made the deal final yet?"

"I know, and this has nothing to do with Mr. Gray."

"What do you mean, Josh?"

"Well, you see, I . . . well, I . . . have you ever wanted something so bad that you were willing to do anything for it? I mean anything. Well, I . . . guess that's what . . ."

"But what does this have to do with you? I'm almost afraid to ask this, but does this have anything to do with your new gift?"

He looked hard into his sister's eyes. He knew that he needed to tell someone, but he never figured that it would be the one sister that he couldn't stand. Josh gestured to his sister with his hands, with tears in his eyes and a cracking voice as the door swung closed. Then the door swung open again with great force. His sister dashed out, yelling for her mother and father.

"Mom! Dad! Oh shit!" yelled his sister as she ran to meet her parents. You could hear a slap come from the living room, and seconds later, she gave a howl. Minutes later his father and mother came into the room where Josh was sitting and closed the door. Minutes seemed like hours, and finally the door swung open again as Josh's father yelled to his wife to stay with Josh until he got back.

As their father headed for the door, he looked at Josh and said, "I hope that I can pull us out of this hole that you have put us in, Boy."

"Don't blame him."

"If not him, then who? It wasn't me that made a pact with the devil!"

"Honey! You don't understand! We pushed him to this, and we gave him no way out either."

"What the he . . ." he stopped himself short and looked at her, whispering, "Sorry." Then he continued, "What are you talking about, Woman?"

"You know what I mean. When was the last time you took your boy fishing? Never. What about camping or hunting? Never. So don't go blaming him because we weren't there for him in the first place. Now go. You girls go to Miss Thompkin's house next door and tell her we'll come by later to get you, because we have an emergency right now."

Josh's little sister looked at him with a scared face and asked, "Are you going to be all right?"

Josh replied, "I don't know yet, but go with the rest of them, and I'll see you later."

His little sister pulled away. She was holding back the tears as hard as she could. It was a battle that she knew that she couldn't win.

Hours later, Josh's father was yelling from the truck telling Josh and his mother to get in.

The door closed, and Josh's mother turned to her husband, and asked, "Where are we going?"

"Well, if I have any say in this, it won't be to hell." The truck sped off as the dirt and dust from the road was mixed in the backdraft of the trucks' tires.

One hour later, the truck stopped in front of an old beat-up farm house.

"Where are we?" asked Mother.

"We're at the old Dubois home."

"Not that old crazy woman."

"Yep! That's the one. Hey! I'm fresh out of ideas unless you can come up with a winner."

The couple looked at each other as silence washed over them for a few minutes. The father reached for Josh's hand and, as if Josh was reading his father's mind, he reached up and grabbed his father's hand. Once they reached the door, the father gave two strong knocks on the door. For a few minutes, nothing happened. He looked back at his wife, and she told him to go ahead, and try again. He reached up to knock once more. As soon as he approached the door with his hand, the door flung open. They heard a voice from the shadows beckoning them to come into the room. Josh had never been this scared before. Not even when his parents came home early one day and found him in his sisters' room wearing their clothes. He couldn't sit down for a week after his father was finished with him. This time he was in a pickle far worse than anything he had ever been in. Josh stood there in the shadow of his father, while his father called out for the old woman.

"Look here. Me and my family need some help, and well, I figured that you are our only hope."

The old woman stepped out of the shadows, and as she approached the boy, she lunged back yelling, "Get out!"

The father replied, "But my boy needs you. He has got himself in a horrible mess."

"I know!" cried out the woman. "That's why I want you and him out of here."

"Look, I was told that you could help people and right now, we need your help."

She paused, and then she looked back into the shadow. "I can see a dark glow around the boy. He has taken a path that holds an eternal price. It's a journey in which if he's not careful, he could never return from."

The old woman looked toward Mother, only to see the sadness and the ashed stream that had dried under her eyes. The old woman looked back at Josh and she said, "Only a true heart and true love can prevail. Look deep inside your soul and find the love that shines from you. That's the only chance you will have."

"Say what? How's that bullshit going to help my boy?"

"What are you expecting from me? There is nothing more that I can do. I've done all that I can."

"Well, to be honest a lot more than . . . that shit! Damn, you are the witch doctor! Isn't there a spell that you can cast? Some magic dust that you can give us, or something to leave with quickly?" He backed up toward the door, stormed out, and returned to the truck, yelling for Josh and his mother to get in. Then he turned to look at the old woman. Mother just smiled as said thanks with a whisper of her voice.

Later, they returned back to the house. The father stayed in the truck and turned to his wife, saying, "I will be back."

Then he spun off, kicking up dirt from the road. Josh walked out of the house through the back door. Like always, he went straight to the barn. He was moving his lips as if he was saying a prayer. Josh had stopped praying a few months back. He felt like no one was listening to his prayers, so he figured that there was no need to pray. He didn't know why, but now he had a strange feeling that maybe someone was listening. The only thing that he was wondering about now was if someone was listening and whether they would help. Josh pulled back the barn door as if someone was in it. Josh was thinking that he should stay out there and wait until it was time. Josh always wanted the gift that was given, but not like this. He wanted to feel and share it, not abuse it like he has seen other stars do. All he wanted to do was to sing and enjoy the music from his voice. Josh thought about all the trouble that he had to face, trying to get the only thing that really mattered to him.

He felt that he had suffered long enough. He thought about all the pain that he was going through just to sing. All of a sudden, Josh felt himself get mad and he couldn't believe that all of this was happening to him.

Josh turned to the dark part of the barn and yelled, "I'm not giving up without a fight! You hear me? I'm not just going to lay down for this. You better be listening to me."

Suddenly, the barn got quiet and Josh felt silly talking to himself. He closed the barn door as he headed for the barn loft. He lay down and turned over to feel himself drifting to sleep. Soon Josh was off in slumberland. A dark figure arose from the dark part of the barn, where Josh had been yelling toward. Strange as it may seem, Josh woke up to see that it was already dark. So he got up and climbed down from the loft and headed for the barn door. As he reached for the door, he noticed the barn light begin to turn red. He was too afraid to turn around and see where the light was coming from. He knew that he had no choice, because his curiosity had gotten the best of him. Josh turned slowly as he looked up only to find that the light bulb had turned red. Josh fell back against a stack of hay and gave a sigh. As soon as he turned back around, he was startled to see the stranger in the red shirt looking at him.

"What's the matter? I thought that was a great speech that you gave earlier, but unfortunately, my boss feels that you went overboard with it, and now, get this part, he is really hot. I mean he is really red in the face. Ha-ha, boy, I really burn me up. Ha-ha. Hey, I did another one. Really, Josh, I know that you are scared shitless, but you'll get over it. Honestly you will. Trust me, but for now we have an appointment with my boss."

"No! Wait a minute." Josh turned to the door to see his father had returned with Pastor Robert. The pastor, his mother, and father approached the man in the red shirt. His eyes turned red and, all of sudden, his father and mother, along with the pastor, just froze in their tracks when the light hit his face, changing his face to a hideous creature.

"This is between me and the boy! Oh, yes. Josh it's time."

"Wait! Please take me, not my boy. Look he's still young. For God's sake take me, you son of a bitch!"

"No! No! I'm sorry, but I just can't do that."

"Look, all I want is for my boy to live."

"So do I!" yelled the mother. "I want to take his place. You can't take my son. Please! You must have known what it must be like to be human once! Please, just remember."

"Well, I tell you what. This is what I will do. If Josh could prove himself, I will release him from his deal, but if he fails, I will take all of you."

They all looked at each other, and his father said, "Please take me. Only me."

"Nope, I'm sorry. No can do. The deal is for all or just the boy. Take it or leave it. You have ten seconds."

Mother looked at her husband and said, "We don't need ten seconds."

Josh yelled out, "No! Not them, just me. Only me! Mom! Dad! I don't want you to suffer for what I've done."

"I'm sorry, Josh, but you don't have a say in this. I already have you, but your parents are an additional bonus."

"What about me?" asked the pastor.

"Pastor, this is between my family and me," replied Josh's father, "so you can leave."

"No. I'm part of your family. What kind of a pastor would I be if I ran? Where would my faith be? No, brother and sister, I'm here for the full length of it."

"Listen, Josh, I believe in you, and your parents believe in you. We know that you can do it. Your parents' lives are in your hands."

"Oh, great! This can't get any better. I get to bring home the big bonus! A preacher! Boy this is great! Four for the price of one. Okay, gang, this is how we are going to do this."

He looked at Josh and his eyes started to glow. They could see a light grow stronger around the barn, and then it stopped. There was a glowing figure standing in the middle of the barn. When their eyes focused, they could see a beautiful woman dressed in all white.

She walked over to the man in the red shirt and said, "You broke the rules, and you didn't think we would be watching. What made you think we would let you get away with this?"

"With what? With what?" screamed the man in the red shirt.

"You know the rules. The child hasn't reached the age of awareness. So you approached this child illegally."

The woman in white walked over to Josh and his parents. She smiled at Josh.

"It's a strange mess you got yourself into, Josh."

"Yes, ma'am." Josh's mother turned to the lady in white and asked if he broke the rules, then Josh is free and clear.

"It's not that simple. It would had been clear if you and your husband and pastor did not attach your souls to the contact, and since you're a legal age of awareness, you made the contract valid, not Josh. Josh is a child."

The mother cried out, "That's right in the Bible that he's not of age yet!"

"But there's a chance. Josh there's something inside of you that has been there all along. Instead of looking at other people's talent, look at yours. It's there. Have faith in yourself. Your parents and pastor do, or they would not be putting their life, soul, and heart on the line for you."

Josh looked over at his family and seeing them smiling at him gave him comfort.

"You okay, Josh? Let's see what you can do."

"No!" Josh cried out to the stranger.

"No help ye shall seek."

Then Josh walked to the edge of the barn door, and he looked at the star-filled sky, and wondered if he had a chance. Josh now realized that he was going have to do this and that he wasn't alone. He realized what he should have done all along. No, he wanted the easy way out. So he had someone else do the dirty work, but it came at a price which he could not afford. Now it was time for him to pay the piper. Josh stared into the night, whispering a few words as he gathered his wit and his strength. Josh's mother and father noticed that he was crying, but they didn't see that his hand was bleeding due to him clenching his hand so tight that his fingernails dug too deep into the palm of his hand. Josh looked at the stranger with a swift turn and his mouth opened and the first note rattled the barn walls. Every note after that caused the night to be silent, as if every creature had to listen to the sweet melodies that flowed from Josh's heart. It seemed as if an angel was singing with Josh. For the first time, he knew that it didn't have anything to do with being born with the talent. It had to come from within—from a pure heart. It was his true heart and his true love that would get him out of this. When Josh was finished, silence settled over the barn. You could feel a warm feeling as it filled the barn.

"Well, Josh, I can honestly say that you won fair and square. You did it without any help or any trickery. And that I can respect, but don't think that this will be the last time that you will see, because I will be watching you. So, for now, it's so long. Just remember I'll be back, because I don't like to lose."

A dark shadow appeared like the shape of a door. The stranger stepped one leg into the door, and then stopped briefly to say, "Before I leave there's an old saying I'll share. 'Once you've been brushed by evil, evil ye shall be.'" He smiled as he finally stepped through the dark void, and the stranger was gone. The pastor and parents turned to find the lady in white, but she also was gone.

But there was a voice softly saying, "Stay strong, Josh, and anymore violations will be met with drastic penalties."

Josh's parents and the pastor ran to embrace Josh.

The pastor screamed, "Praise the Lord" several times.

Josh's father was in shock. He kept asking, "What has happened? Don't get me wrong, I'm glad that it turned out in our favor, but how and . . . ?"

The pastor turned to Josh's father and said, "Faith as a grain of a mustard seed (Matthew 17:20)." He grasped the Bible tighter and smiled. "He found his faith, his true calling, his savior, and it's Jesus."

As his mother called out to him and told him that everything was fine, Josh didn't turn around so his mother asked him what was wrong. Still, they couldn't get Josh to talk. Josh tried to open his mouth and say something, but nothing came out.

Josh's mother yelled out with a scream, and said, "He can't talk."

"Oh my, oh my," Josh replied with a scratchy voice. He paid with the only thing that almost meant more to him then his soul—his voice. Everyone was thinking of the last statement that the man made before he left, wondering what the stranger meant by that last remark.

Josh was saved, but at a cost.

The scene fades as his mother holds him.

***

Twenty years later, we see a man enter a church full of people. He walks to the front of the church to stand next to a coffin with a body. The person in the coffin is Josh's mother, and the man standing next to her coffin is her son Josh. Josh leans over and smiles at his mother's body for a second. He grabs her cold lifeless hand and squeezes it. Josh turns and sits with the rest of his siblings.

Josh looks to his left at the empty seat next to him, thinking about his father who passed away a few years back. Josh had not spoken a word since that cold weird night in the barn. No one knew why or ever asked. They only knew that a miracle had taken place and not to push fate to question it. It was best to leave it alone. The pastor came to the podium and started the service.

As the pastor began to talk about his mother, the good deeds that she did and the great love the community had for her, Josh started to flash back to the time at the old home. He came back to reality when he heard his sister's name called to the podium. He was confused until he looked at the program and saw that she was to sing. He smiled and looked at her as she walked to the front of the podium. The music began and his sister opened her mouth, then covered her face and began to cry. She wiped her face and motioned the music to start again. The music once again started to play but once again she couldn't sing and pulled away from the mic. She started to turn and walk away when she felt a hand on her shoulder stop her. She looked up, wiped her tears, and noticed it was Josh. Josh smiled and nudged her to the microphone. Josh motioned the music to begin. There was a short pause and suddenly the music started again. But this time Josh held her hand tight, and he began singing, holding his sister close. The church was in shock as Josh's voice rang out in the building, with a strong and deep force. He was singing one of his mother's favorite songs, "I'm Going Away."

Everyone was standing on their feet as Josh gave the best performance of his life for the woman who gave him life. A few people wondered what the big deal was of a young man singing as people whispered that Josh hadn't spoken a word for more than twenty years. Josh looked down into his mother's coffin as he reached the high notes of the song. He gestured his sister to take over. She did, and she give a great performance.

Josh joined in, and for the next hour, they both are outstanding. Suddenly Josh started to feel dizzy, he grabbed on to the podium for support. Josh collapsed on the floor next to the coffin. The people ran to Josh's aid to help him. You could see Josh's right hand still clinging to the edge of his mother's coffin. Josh tried to regain his balance and focused his eyes on what was about to happen to next.

As the door of the church swung open and closed as people entered and exited to see what was going on in the church, Josh could see a dark figure, a man standing across the street looking at him through the doors of the church. The man was smiling. Josh was trying to say something, but was unable to speak. Falling again to the floor and gasping for air as he grabbed his throat, his eyes glossed over as he tried to stay focused on the figure standing across the street. But no one was paying attention to what Josh was trying to point out. Still, the dark stranger was standing there smiling, and everyone was yelling and running to help Josh. Suddenly the stranger came into focus.

The man was wearing black trousers and a bright red shirt with black buttons down the left side of the shirt. Josh's eyes adjusted, and he could see who the stranger was. He pointed and grunted. No one paid him any attention and continued to seek medical attention for Josh, except his sister, Beverly, who looked where Josh was pointing. Beverly felt a cold chill over her spine as she fell back against the bench and started crying. She saw the man, and the man noticed her. He stepped off the curb and began to walk toward the church door. As he tried to step up to the curb that led to the church, something stopped him, like an invisible wall keeping him still or preventing him from moving forward. No matter how many times he tried, he couldn't move forward. He finally stopped, looked up, snarled, and then smiled. He turned to Josh and his sister Beverly. With a smile, he tipped his hat and vanished.

Josh looked at his sister Beverly and smiled. She whispered, "It's okay. He's gone. He won't be back. I promise. I know I believed Mommy asked God to watch over us." She smiled too.

Josh whispered, "I love you, Sis," and he passed out.

The family was in the hospital room surrounding Josh's bed, giving him support. Everyone was talking at the same time, trying to find out how was he able to sing after all these years, and why he had a hard time breathing in the church. All of a sudden, the doctor came in the room and the noise stopped. Everyone looked toward the doctor as he walked toward Josh's bedside. The doctor smiled as he grabbed Josh's arm and told him the result of the test.

"Josh, we ran all the tests we could. It seems that your vocal cords were severed years ago."

The room became silent, and everyone looked at each other without saying a word.

Then the silence was broken with one of Josh's sister saying in a stuttering voice, "That's not possible, Doctor. Josh just sang today at church, at our mother's funeral."

The doctor turned to the family. "I can't see how that can be since the tests told another story. His vocals are damaged and severed. There's no way he could talk or sing. I would like to keep Josh overnight for observation. He can go home in the morning." The doctor exited the room.

A young man yelled out, "Wait a minute! I have it on my phone. That's right. I recorded it on my phone."

As he pulled up the footage, he noticed that it showed all he had recorded except the footage of Josh singing. All he had of that was snow. As the room became quiet, everyone looked at Josh as Josh smiled and pulled the covers over him. The faces in the room were stunned and shocked. The room faded as Josh looked up just smiling.

***

Thirty-five years had past, and there's an old man sitting in a living room looking out the window as a woman calls him for dinner. He sits at the table with her, some children, and her husband. The husband gives the dinner prayer. The little girl on the old man's right side leans over and tells him that she prayed that one day he would give the dinner prayer. Her father looks at the daughter out the corner of his eyes and clears his throat to get her attention.

"Now let her be, honey," replied her mother. "But Beverly that's not how we raised our children."

"Look, honey," he directed his remark to the little girl, "Uncle Josh can never talk, but he does appreciate it, okay, baby."

"Yes, Daddy." Josh looked at the girl and smiled. He wondered what would happen if he had kids. But he knows that will never happen because he remembered what the stranger had said forty-five years ago in that cold night in that barn.

"Once you've been brushed by evil, evil ye shall be."

He feared that if he ever had children, he would hand down his sinful crime, but he looked around and with a smile, he saw that he had enough children. They were all that he will ever need.

Later that evening, Josh's little niece was off in a room by herself singing, and her singing is beautiful and sweet. In the corner of the room, just below the shadow of the light, you see a dark figure standing, looking at the girl with a sinister look on his face. Standing, thinking, and smiling.

The man with the red shirt started to walk toward the door, saying in a low tone, "Oh, she'll do just fine, just fine as . . ." He laughed.

There was a loud thunderous noise as the man with the red shirt looked up and screamed from a lightning bolt strike. All you could see was smoke. The room lit up. She stopped and looking toward the smoke.

She said, "No, sir, I won't do fine." With a smile, she turned and continued to play.

A voice coming out of the air said, "We told you once, and once is all we need to tell you."

Review Requested:

If you loved this book, would you please provide
a review at Amazon.com?

CPSIA information can be obtained
at www.ICGtesting.com
Printed in the USA
LVHW040143230719
624964LV00001B/310/P